Marvellous Poets

Edited By Jenni Harrison

First published in Great Britain in 2020 by:

Young Writers
Remus House
Coltsfoot Drive
Peterborough
PE2 9BF
Telephone: 01733 890066
Website: www.youngwriters.co.uk

All Rights Reserved
Book Design by Ashley Janson
© Copyright Contributors 2020
Softback ISBN 978-1-80015-034-8

Printed and bound in the UK by BookPrintingUK
Website: www.bookprintinguk.com
YB0448A

FOREWORD

Here at Young Writers our defining aim is to promote the joys of reading and writing to children and young adults and we are committed to nurturing the creative talents of the next generation. By allowing them to see their own work in print we believe their confidence and love of creative writing will grow.

Out Of This World is our latest fantastic competition, specifically designed to encourage the writing skills of primary school children through the medium of poetry. From the high quality of entries received, it is clear that it really captured the imagination of all involved.

We are proud to present the resulting collection of poems that we are sure will amuse and inspire.

An absorbing insight into the imagination and thoughts of the young, we hope you will agree that this fantastic anthology is one to delight the whole family again and again.

CONTENTS

Broad Heath Community Primary School, Coventry

Mahamad Yousif (11)	1
Ayesha Gray (11)	2

Burry Port Community School, Burry Port

Lennon Webb (9)	4
Cai Mpofu (9)	5
Ebony Phillips (8)	6
Gaby Bowley (8)	7
Ellie Thomas (9)	8
LillyBeau Howell (8)	9
Lily T (9), Tyler & Mia	10
Levi Brady Rees (9)	11
Gia Davies (8)	12
Levi Rose (9)	13
Harry Webb (9)	14

Corpus Christi RC Primary School, Birmingham

Carys Smith-Reid (8)	15
Inaya Nadeem (11)	16
Connie-Louise Richardson (11)	18

Edward Wilson Primary School, Westminster

Abbas Mohsen (11)	19
Imran Arbab (10)	20
Shakila Jackson (11)	24
Ben Fay (7)	26
Laila Youssef (9)	28
Dania El-Turabi (11)	30

Ibrahim Arbab (8)	32
Jannah Sumaya (10)	33
Noor Al-Tayeb (9)	34
Hussein Ghanem (7)	35
Allya Rashid (11)	36
I A (9)	37
Fatima Zahra Dergoul (7)	38
Nora Taleb (11)	39
Anis Taleb (8)	40
Jihad Charem (11)	41
Roqayah Al Memar (9)	42
Berna Gashi (8)	43
Ignacio Carvajal (10)	44
Yousif Qazizada (9)	45
Abrar Benserghin (10)	46
Marwa Haffaf (9)	47
Zubaydah Aktar (9)	48
Rozjanne Sheriff (8)	49
Mais El-Zarif (9)	50
Maryam Mirza (7)	51

Lingfield Primary School, Lingfield

Elspeth Ely (7)	52
Neve Kitley-Spencer (7)	53
Sachin Patel (7)	54
Sofia Hunt (7)	55
Oliver Webb (6)	56

Norfolk House School, Edgbaston

Levizah Hassan-Smith (6) & Leonie-Marie	57

Oak Field Primary School, Gibbonsdown

Lacie White (8)	58
Sienna Nash (8)	59
Kerriann Hopkins (9)	60
Briar-Rose McDonnell (9)	61
Chloe Froud (8)	62
Jessica Magrin (9)	63
Josh O'Connell (8)	64
Evelyn North (9)	65
Owen Berrow (8)	66

Shirenewton Primary School, Shirenewton

Terah Rose Parkhouse (10)	67

St Felix Preparatory School, Reydon

Toby West (10)	68
Samuel Parle (11)	69
Henry O'Connor (9)	70
Charlotte Rainer (10)	71
Alex Drake (11)	72
Samuel Barker-Harrison (11)	74
Eva Bullion (10)	75
William Foskett (11)	76
Saffron Vine (11)	77
Grace Cadey (11)	78
John Pitt (9)	79
Chloe Partridge (10)	80
Bryce Newman (9)	81
William Last (10)	82
Jude Gunner (10)	83
Jude Groom (10)	84
Darcey Impson (9)	85
Darcey McDonough (11)	86
Ben Every (11)	87
Holly Wilson (9)	88

St Michael & St John's RC Primary School, Clitheroe

Mike Tomlein (9)	89

Stifford Clays Primary School, Stifford Clays

Sofia Roche (7)	91
Iris Clark (8)	92
Lily Yuen (7)	93
Ava Coldwell (7)	94

Twycross House School, Twycross

Olivia O'Brien (11)	95
Martha Bettley (11) & Victoria Hudson	96
Alessandra Beck (11)	98
Isabelle Randle (10)	99
Violet Stacey (11)	100
Scarlett Tombs (11)	101
Amelia Carthy	102
Clara Taviner-Hodge (10)	103

Walgrave Primary School, Walgrave

Sycamore Class	104
Lily Knight (10)	106
Joseph Ludwig (9)	107
Sophie Holmes (9)	108
Ellie Brown (10)	109
Harvey Singh Hammond (9)	110

Weald Rise Primary School, Harrow Weald

Manal Mohamed Hilmy (10)	111
Shamsa Abdalla (10)	112
Patricia Sterchevici (9)	113
Khadeeja Fairoos (10)	114
Rikza Mohamed Mohamed Rikas (9)	115
Ayesha Mohamed Fairoos (8)	116

Ysgol Borthyn, Ruthin

Katelyn Beaumont (9)	117
Caitlyn Spencer (9)	118

Ysgol Bro Aled, Llansannan

Jasmine Rose Murray (9)	119

Ysgol Cae'r Nant, Connahs Quay

Alfie Howells (11)	120
Holly Crossley (11)	122
Ella Leverton (10)	123

Ysgol Garth Olwg, Church Village

Jennifer Lewis (8)	124

Ysgol Gynradd Gymraeg Caerffili, Caerphilly

Ffion-Jane Enoch	125

Ysgol Llywelyn, Rhyl

Roan Oakley (11)	126
Kayleigh Roberts (11)	128
Olivia Muller (10)	130
Emma Watkiss (11)	131
Evie Collier (10)	132
Callum Mannion (11)	133
Ruby Hartley (11)	134
Teagan Jones (11)	135
Lucy Bamford (11)	136
Madison Parr (10)	137
Bailey Ellis (10)	138
Josh Hamilton (11)	139
Mia Jones (11)	140
Jake Lamb (10)	141
Warren Wold (10)	142
Huw Espley (11)	143

Ysgol Melyd, Prestatyn

Nia Benson (11)	144
Benjamin Hannah (10)	146
Ethan Duffy Hamill (10)	148
Violet O'Neill (9)	149
Summer Eastwood (11)	150
Lily Adams (10)	151
Natarlia Stojkovska (11)	152
Ben Hughes (11)	154
Bella Bennett (10)	155
Theo Haywood (10)	156
Oliver Aspinwall (11)	157
Iwan Miles (10)	158
Louis Jones (10)	159

Ysgol Pum Heol, Llanelli

Isobel Jane Pellew (11)	160
Oliver Manning (8)	161
Cadi Fflur DeSouza (11)	162
Eiry Bailey (8)	164

Ysgol Wepre School, Connah's Quay

Silvija Liuzinaite (11)	165
Charlotte Sprake (11)	166
Sebastian Randles (11)	167

THE POEMS

Universe 99

There once was race named Superior
There was once a race named Inferior
Superior held Inferior hostage
Though at a huge costage
They were linked by the white wormhole
But Superior had a sneaky mole
He was a faithful Inferior spy
He would never hurt a fly
This took place in Universe 99
The spy was at the sacrificing shrine
Superiors were reluctantly donated to
John the superhuman carefully drew
His plans would be completely foolproof
It had been decided by fate
He would get help from his mate
After his rewarded efforts, he decided to dine
And that is the beginning of the story of Universe 99.

Mahamad Yousif (11)
Broad Heath Community Primary School, Coventry

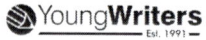

Earth

Space, space, isn't it ace?
With its pitch-black sky
Shame there is no other life
Well, that's a lie
There are...
The residents of Planet Zog
Whose planet is engulfed in fog
Their favourite food?
Why a log!
Cos these are the residents of Planet Zog

Then there are the locals on Planet Gee
I'm from Planet Gee, me!
Can't you see
We always love our green tea
So...
Give us a cuppa and leave us be

We couldn't leave out Planet O
They're always in a rush, so sorry they had to go
Now let's take a look at Planet Ook

These aliens always have their noses stuck in
a book
They were recently invaded by Planet Mook
Who took the liberty of shocking everything until
the planet shook!

So now our trip into space is drawing to an end
But there's this one thing that drives me round
the bend
I never introduced you to a new planet called Earth
The aliens there are warming their planet like
a hearth
They're not taking care of it at all
At this rate the whole civilisation will fall
Then they wonder why we don't tell them
we're here
For it is their ruthlessness we fear.

Ayesha Gray (11)
Broad Heath Community Primary School, Coventry

Neil Armstrong

Neil Armstrong was first on the moon, he slept in the afternoon.
Apollo 11 was his rocket ship, they took an amazing trip.
Buzz Aldrin was his partner and he slept after.
The rocket was going to explode, they had to enter a code.
They were cold, a partner was bold.

Neil Armstrong was first on the moon, he slept in the afternoon.
His ship, Apollo 11, played a good tune.
His partner was cold and then turned to mould.
He was being weird, that's what he got told.
Then he spotted a racoon!

Lennon Webb (9)
Burry Port Community School, Burry Port

Having A Great Day

There was a girl named Ray
Who had a very good day
She found her enemy Kylo Ren
Who looked for wise men
She was a fan of Santa's sleigh.

There was a man who went to space
Who saw a peculiar place
He went to see friends
But kept on seeing pens
He had a very competitive race.

There was an alien named Pat
Who liked wearing hats
He took one off
Then had a big cough
He wanted to play with a rat.

Cai Mpofu (9)
Burry Port Community School, Burry Port

Neptune

There once was a little blue planet
It was a little cold and it saw a giant Janet
It was really cool in space
It saw an alien winning a race
Then an astronaut came by and saw the planet.

There once was a dark cave
With an alien who was very brave
Then they saw a rocket
So they checked in their pockets
And met the alien called Dave.

Ebony Phillips (8)
Burry Port Community School, Burry Port

The Lady On The Moon/The Happy Moon

There once was a lady called Molly
And she had a friend called Olly
They got in a hot-air balloon
And flew over the moon
Then they were lost and sad, "Oh golly!"

There was a moon called Tom
And Ellie was his mom
They lived by Mars
Amongst the stars
Then they went to prom!

Gaby Bowley (8)
Burry Port Community School, Burry Port

Out To Space

There once was a girl called Trace
And she went to space
She went in her rocket
That was in her pocket
And she was in a completely different place!

There once was an alien called Bob
He had a pet dog
He went to space with Grace
To a different place
And he went for a jog!

Ellie Thomas (9)
Burry Port Community School, Burry Port

Alien And Moon

Once there was an alien
He went to the stadium
He missed the game
And went home to blame
The gymnasium.

Once there was a talking moon
He was a goon
He had no nose
He had a dog called Rose
He had a balloon.

LillyBeau Howell (8)
Burry Port Community School, Burry Port

Space Race

A rocket full of animals went to space
They drove go-karts in a race
An alien came to watch them play
They played and played till the end of the day
They got back in the rocket with a smile on their face.

Lily T (9), Tyler & Mia
Burry Port Community School, Burry Port

The Man On The Moon

There once was a man on the moon
Who was watching his favourite cartoon
Who looked down on Earth
At the planet of his birth
Looking for a place for his honeymoon.

Levi Brady Rees (9)
Burry Port Community School, Burry Port

Molly Is Jolly

There was a lady and her name was Molly
She was very, very jolly
She had a very big ear
Then her friend said, "Come here!"
This friend was called Holly.

Gia Davies (8)
Burry Port Community School, Burry Port

The Cutie

There was a little baby called Yoda
He always drank lime soda
He trained a Jedi
Who nearly had two red eyes
Yoda was wise and good at yoga!

Levi Rose (9)
Burry Port Community School, Burry Port

The Alien Who Always Reports

There once was an alien, he name was Alex
He liked to eat metallics
He hated sport
But he always did report
And he wrote in italics!

Harry Webb (9)
Burry Port Community School, Burry Port

Shining Light

In the sky I fly
Like a bird far and high

So great, so high
I am in the sky

A shining light
So far and bright

But a burning light gives me a fright
For it will soon be light

And it's such a delight!

Carys Smith-Reid (8)
Corpus Christi RC Primary School, Birmingham

Andy And Alan

Andy waited for night to fall,
So he could climb into his rocket and explore.
The sights and sounds of space in all its glory
"Come on sky, get darker, I'm in a hurry."

Darkness came and off went Andy
He took some snacks and drinks, they would be handy.
Up he went going past stars so bright
Shining and glittering, there was so much light.

The planets were spinning round and round,
"Oh how many more planets could be found?"
Suddenly a figure stood on top of Saturn
It was an alien and he said, "Hello, I'm Alan!

I'm your friend in space, I'm green and have a round tummy
I would love to be your friend, I'm kind and funny"

Andy and Alan are now mates, each wearing a smile their face,
Time for many adventures, watch this space!

Inaya Nadeem (11)
Corpus Christi RC Primary School, Birmingham

My Baby Boy Cass

C razy Cass he is
A little nutter
S o cute indeed
S o much I love him.

Connie-Louise Richardson (11)
Corpus Christi RC Primary School, Birmingham

Hell's Overlord

Mortus Vincula
He is Hell's ruler
Many facts about him are unknown
Talk rubbish and across Hell you'd be thrown
And trust me you'll get more than one wound
Then he'll bury you alive in your grey tomb
And when you're dead, he still won't stop
He'll crack all your bones till they pop

Mortus isn't always physical, he sometimes feeds on fear
As he loves to see his foes incur loads of tears
He shows deceased relatives until you're shaken to the core
And as you try to forget what you saw
You have an emotional breakdown
So sad, it's impossible not to frown
Mortus Vincula
He is Hell's ruler.

Abbas Mohsen (11)
Edward Wilson Primary School, Westminster

What Lies In Space

Far, far away
149 million kilometres away
Rests the universe's most extraordinary object
The one and only solar system!

The sun
The heart of our solar system,
Without it we would not be alive
Crackling and burning away
It nourishes everything in a way
When the sun elevates into the sky
The world smiles, even the flowers

Mercury
So nice and soft
It is the sixth planet and sends the wind aloft
When the stars are warm
It's just burning hot
But it is just as cold when they are not
Mercury is so similar to its friends the stars but
Mercury is made of rock and they are not

Venus
Second planet from the sun
Named after the Roman goddess of love
Just for fun it spins clockwise
And is the brightest object in the skies

Earth
Third planet from the sun
We all live on it and it is really fun
It has a moon that is 385km away
Compared to the other planets it has way less.

Mars
The ancients called it Ares
But now we call it Mars
It is as red as the blood shed during wars
The sandstorms are bigger than anywhere else
Mars is filled with craters, asteroids and the biggest volcano, Olympus Mons

Jupiter
Fifth planet from the sun
It has 57 moons
And has not had a storm since the 17th century

It might look like a big ball of gas
But it's quite a nice accessory to the solar system

Saturn
The planet with the amazing rings
Made out of a lake of things
Beautiful Saturn gleaming in the night sky
Glistening brightly as time flies by
Its rings are not diamonds but are still quite nice

Uranus
It spins on its side
And faces upside down
This planet can never stand straight
Which is really not fun
It's the seventh planet from the sun
87 years it takes it to go round the sun
So that's most of your lifetime gone!

Neptune
So far away from the sun
It is really not fun
-201 degrees is the temperature
That is way colder than Antarctica

Pluto
The planet that got lost
When it came back
It transformed into a dwarf planet
And never went back
So now Neptune is last.

Imran Arbab (10)
Edward Wilson Primary School, Westminster

Life

Running out of time, losing my mind
Excited but lost, perseverance is a must
We add and subtract and try not to look back
No time for division with all the revision
The numbers are adding up, but we are still losing time
And this puts stress on our minds
No time for living because of this vision that has been laid by the system
Water the plants but they left the sprinklers running
Now we are flooding with all sorts
It won't stop, now we need the mop
Soak it up till dry, the truth will never lie
You will see it for yourself, ever been on a ride called 'stealth'?
Well buckle up for this ride called 'life'
Where we are always running for time

Wait for the stop sign or the finish line
But time doesn't stop, it's a forever clock
Just don't be shocked
Use time wisely.

Shakila Jackson (11)
Edward Wilson Primary School, Westminster

Ghost Train

I feel like I've just boarded a ghost train
The lights are dimmed and I'm feeling kind of strange
I feel like I've just boarded a ghost train
Next stop 58th street and the Avenue of Sange

I went down to Coney Island
Bought myself a dirty water dog
For lunch I feasted on a tasty meal
Of good old rice and hog

I went down to Coney Island
Went to see the Cyclones play
I watched them almost beat the Yankees
But that will have to be another day

Went back to the station
Took the F train home
Luckily I don't live far away
Good thing I don't live in Rome

It turns out this ghost train wasn't real
It was all just part of my dreams
Because when I woke up this morning
I was greeted by sunbeams.

Ben Fay (7)
Edward Wilson Primary School, Westminster

Something To Be Afraid Of!

I hear them tell the witches to run around on Halloween,
But though I've been almost everywhere, no witches have I seen.
Of course, I've seen some girls made up to look like witches, eerie,
But, huh, I knew them, every one when they came near me.
They tell about the ghosts that stalk, so white and slim and tall,
But I know who the fellows are and where they live and all.
And jack o' lanterns, they are just some pumpkins big, dug out,
Then candles put inside to make the light shine about.
And goblins, they are made-up too, just boys from our school,
If I should run from them I'd think I was a fool.

And so I cannot see at all why people should run,
Or be afraid of spooky things which are just made for fun.

Laila Youssef (9)
Edward Wilson Primary School, Westminster

Bailey

Bailey, Bailey
Casually walking on the street
Bailey, Bailey
Has no one to meet

Bailey, Bailey
Sees a strange creature
Bailey, Bailey
Notices its strange features

Bailey, Bailey
She talks to it
It doesn't want to reply
Not even a bit

Bailey, Bailey
Looks at its huge eyes
Its strange large face
She has nothing to despise

At last it speaks
"Want to be friends?" it asks

Bailey is confused
But replies with a yes

Bailey, Bailey
She's finally found a friend
"Are we best friends?" the creature asks
"Till the end," Bailey says.

Dania El-Turabi (11)
Edward Wilson Primary School, Westminster

The Solar System

Look up at the beautiful sun made from nature
The sun is so bright and powerful
It brings light to the Earth in minutes
Without it all our flowers would be dead
The moon shines light to the Earth
Earth, but not like the sun

The moon is like an enormous clock in the air
The moon doesn't always look the same, it changes shape every night
All of the things that belong to the day are fast asleep

Stars shine light to the Earth day and night
They might look like round balls in the sky
You might see the beautiful stars in the sky at night
The stars shine to the Earth the same time as the moon does.

Ibrahim Arbab (8)
Edward Wilson Primary School, Westminster

Just Dreams

A relaxing lie-down can redeem joy, happiness and
Memories, a gentle ripple travelling through a sea
of murky memories
Closed eyes and a flickering body
Sights, galleries and unknown paths I might come
across
In a visual world of my own on this journey,
Just me in the misty sky, jumping from cloud to
cloud
With a face full of glee, ending up in an
extravagant place
My, my what a sight I see
My thrilling, convincing joy had an abrupt ending
Due to a ding, ding, ding noise here and there
It was an irritating alarm to get ready for my
expedition
All about soon-to-be achieved hopes and dreams.

Jannah Sumaya (10)
Edward Wilson Primary School, Westminster

We're Killing The Earth

We're killing the Earth, that's really not fun
No one believes us because we are young
Our forests are turning to ash in seconds
Ask California they will tell you about it
They will tell you how they have lost their homes
Some people are just doing tweets on their phones
Global warming is killing our home
For the last time this is not a joke
We can't stop putting chemicals in what we are trying to breathe
Our future is stolen and we are the thieves

Dear 2020,
I hope you hear my apology
I've come a long way to say
I'm sorry...

Noor Al-Tayeb (9)
Edward Wilson Primary School, Westminster

The Struggles Of Going To Space

Oh how I love space
I've already packed my suitcase
Oh how I'd love to be there now
But the thing is I don't know how

I could build a spaceship
By starting with a paperclip
Or ride a flying boat
But how can I make it float?

My dreams should stay my dreams
As they are a bit extreme
The thing is I'm only seven
I live in a place called Devon

I can't go to space because it's too far
And I can't see my favourite star
But it will always shine bright
To guide me to it one night.

Hussein Ghanem (7)
Edward Wilson Primary School, Westminster

The Stars And Galaxies

It's good to stretch our minds and study
outer space
Where trillions of stars, a smallness does erase
With light-years in the billions we cannot realise
The vastness of space that all around us lies
All of this vast space in light years so we say
Belongs to only one - it is God's domain
Ruler over space, creator of it too
We can see how vas it is and get another view
The world is how you see it, you're free to choose
your sight
To look for love and goodness or dim your
inner light.

Allya Rashid (11)
Edward Wilson Primary School, Westminster

Land Of The Forgotten

As the wind dances through the trees
An echo screams as loud as can be
Fragile hearts lie between the walls
As emptiness fall through the halls
In this land nothing exists
Yet we can't stop using our fists
The Land of the Forgotten
What you can't control
In your mind
It's deep down below
Our life is rotten, yes I know
Where homes disappear
And, well, lives they can't reappear
No we aren't really alive
Cos you're in the Land of the Forgotten tonight.

I A (9)
Edward Wilson Primary School, Westminster

As The World Changes

As the sun shines in my eyes
The beautiful birds fly by
I smell the beautiful blossoms as I walk by
When I walk by
The soft raspberries I see grow before my eyes
I see my mum place flowers everywhere
Very pretty ones in our house
When it's night-time I look into the sky and see the shining stars
When it's dark I see the wind blowing the trees
I can see outside, it's pitch-black
Earlier in the evening it was raining
Now the leaves are soaking wet.

Fatima Zahra Dergoul (7)
Edward Wilson Primary School, Westminster

The Four Unknown Planets

In a place far away
In a place nobody knew about
Stood four little planets
That looked different in all sorts of ways
One of the planets brought happiness and joy
The other brought sadness and fear
Another made you feel tired and snoozy
Now the last planet has arrived
This planet was the worst of all
If you got trapped there
You would never escape
Now you know about all of the mysterious planets
That stand alone in a pit full of darkness.

Nora Taleb (11)
Edward Wilson Primary School, Westminster

The Secrets Of The Universe

In a land far away
Sat five unknown planets
Each of them were different
In their own special way
One was full of endless toys
The other was filled with endless joy
The third planet was covered in food
Whilst the other one was full of drinks
Now there is only one planet left
The worst one yet
It brings all of your fear and sadness
Making you shake in fright

These are all the unknown planets
That hide from us far, far away.

Anis Taleb (8)
Edward Wilson Primary School, Westminster

The Button!

Tim Peake
Found a leak
He went to fix it
He found a button and eventually clicked it

It took him to space
Where he fell on his face
And he shot up with shock
To find himself upon a block

He shouted and yelped
Waiting for some help
He came across an alien
Who was Australian

It helped him go back in time
And he became a wealthy mime!

Jihad Charem (11)
Edward Wilson Primary School, Westminster

I'm A Lonely Asteroid

I'm a lonely asteroid
Always annoyed
When all the other asteroids
Are enjoyed
All the asteroids play games
Not inviting me because they think I'm weird
Since I'm alone
I like to moan

One day I heard an asteroid gave birth
But the baby accidentally flew to Earth
I flew
I heard a cow go moo
I saved the day
So now I am allowed to play!

Roqayah Al Memar (9)
Edward Wilson Primary School, Westminster

The Iron Man

Where has he come from?
Nobody knows
His torso is as big as a huge bin
His eyes are as bright as the light on a lighthouse
How long had he walked?
Nobody knows
Head as big as a sand bucket
How old is he?
Nobody knows
Feet as thick as a Harry Potter book
His smile is like a gigantic semicircle
Does he have a heart?
Nobody knows
Is he friend or foe…?

Berna Gashi (8)
Edward Wilson Primary School, Westminster

The Shining Stars

How many stars are there in the sky?
Perhaps infinity, we might never know
The sunlight blinds me, so I can't see you all
At night you shine bright, I ask myself why.
With infinite stars, would the sky not be white?
Or just the nearest ones can reach us with their light
I wonder if you're all forever shining bright
Or you just peek at Earth night after night.

Ignacio Carvajal (10)
Edward Wilson Primary School, Westminster

There Is No Planet B!

Our world is turning to dust,
Exactly like a piece of rust,
Saving the Earth is the only way,
To survive and have a dance and play,
We are happy and we are sad,
But later on we will not be glad.
The bridges and buildings are falling down,
Because of us we make pollution on the ground.
I hope we help our Planet A,
Because it may sadly go away.

Yousif Qazizada (9)
Edward Wilson Primary School, Westminster

Four Feathers

My youth club is called Four Feathers
I go there during the week
It is amazing and cool
There's computers and pool
There's a studio in the basement
And much, much more
There's girls' night on Monday
It helps you with your homework and they give you a snack
So that's why I keep going back!

Abrar Benserghin (10)
Edward Wilson Primary School, Westminster

Why Does War Exist?

Why does war exist?
The world doesn't even know about this
But in my eyes it's just another crisis
But the truth is this
We just want peace and bliss
We want war to stop
No more bad cops
No frowns
Just forever have smiles all around.

Marwa Haffaf (9)
Edward Wilson Primary School, Westminster

Jewellery And Its Life

Jewellery shines
Jewellery glimmers in the eye of the sun
Emeralds, sapphires and rubies show the love
in their work
Pearls are the queens of the sea
Life for jewellery is glamorous
It's the word we use for
Jewellery, jewellery, jewellery!

Zubaydah Aktar (9)
Edward Wilson Primary School, Westminster

Good And Bad

Is good, bad?
Never be afraid to try new things
Dare to go out in the dark
Need to know that there's a bark
Be yourself and be good
Don't be evil because you'd be a coward
Every day is your shimmering day!

Rozjanne Sheriff (8)
Edward Wilson Primary School, Westminster

Lollipop, Lollipop

Lollipop, lollipop come to me
I have to eat you, yum yummy!
Blue or red I love it so sweet
I lick it low and eat it slow
Lollipop, lollipop you smell so good
Like a Christmas treat so sweet!
Marvellous lollipops!

Mais El-Zarif (9)
Edward Wilson Primary School, Westminster

Car

I went for a drive in my car
I didn't get very far
I ran out of fuel
And thought that was not cool
I had sunglasses on
And I did a very big yawn
Then I went to bed
And that's all I have said.

Maryam Mirza (7)
Edward Wilson Primary School, Westminster

Out Of This World!

O uter space stars twinkle so brightly
U nicorns dance in the light of the moon
T hunderstorms crash through the universe

O rbiting planets travelling around the scorching sun
F iery Mars so hot and angry

T he largest planet is Jupiter, 11 times bigger than Earth
H overing Saturn with boiling rings
I n outer space brave unicorns and aliens fight
S paceships zoom from Earth to Mercury

W ishing upon a bright shooting star
O xygen left behind on Earth
R ockets whizz to the huge moon
L ook at the magical shooting stars
D arkness reaching out into space.

Elspeth Ely (7)
Lingfield Primary School, Lingfield

Unicorns Up And Away!

The unicorn is as white as the moon,
her face is as bright as the sun,
her eyes are as blue as the sky.

She is fun, go and meet her.

Let's go!

Okay we are on the moon where she lives.

"Hi, I'm Rosy, come in,
Let's go to the moon park!"

We lived happily ever after.

Neve Kitley-Spencer (7)
Lingfield Primary School, Lingfield

Giant Jupiter

J upiter is a giant
U ranus is Jupiter's friend
P erhaps there could be aliens there?
I s it dangerous to go?
T hey might send an invitation to Earth
E arthlings would be thrilled!
R iding around the great red spot!

Sachin Patel (7)
Lingfield Primary School, Lingfield

An Alien Called Mars

An alien came to say hello
The alien's name was Mars
The alien was really sad
And didn't know how to play
He met a girl called Sofia
Who taught him how to play
They played and played together
Until he had to fly away!

Sofia Hunt (7)
Lingfield Primary School, Lingfield

Aliens Attack The Moon

Seven hundred aliens attack the moon
One hundred ninjas come to save the moon
One person gets eaten
I save the moon!

Oliver Webb (6)
Lingfield Primary School, Lingfield

Monsters

M oving and stomping around the wild woods
O ut of clear sight
N asty knobbly knees that wobble
S limy slithering snot coming out of a green, prickly nose
T errifying bloody razor-sharp claws
E ating juicy dead people
R ed eyes like scorching fire
S caly, scratchy monsters creeping around the bubbly, smelly swamp.

Levizah Hassan-Smith (6) & Leonie-Marie
Norfolk House School, Edgbaston

Planets

P luto Is close to Neptune
L and is what people live on
A liens visit Area 51 sometimes
N eptune is the most dark blue planet
E arth is what we live on
T here are eight planets in the solar system
S aturn is famous for its rings.

Lacie White (8)
Oak Field Primary School, Gibbonsdown

Journey To The Moon

Ten...
Nine...
Eight...
Seven...
Six...
Five...
Four...
Three...
Two...
One...
Blast-off!
Sweet relief
The countdown is complete
Rockets booming in the sky
They go up and up
The higher they fly
Taking you to the moon.

Sienna Nash (8)
Oak Field Primary School, Gibbonsdown

Earth

E arth is the planet we live on
A solar system keeps the planets safe
R ight bright stars in the solar system
T he solar system as a big star
H i to our solar system.

Kerriann Hopkins (9)
Oak Field Primary School, Gibbonsdown

Space

S pacecrafts soaring through the sky
P lanets orbiting the sun
A ll around are stars twinkling
C raters on every planet
E verything in space is unique.

Briar-Rose McDonnell (9)
Oak Field Primary School, Gibbonsdown

Alien

Slimy-hider
Tall-walker
Galaxy-traveller
Bug-eyed-frightener
Bald-shooter
Gross-boner
Lizard-learner
Green-glower
That is an alien!

Chloe Froud (8)
Oak Field Primary School, Gibbonsdown

Alien

Scary-slimer
High-jumper
Sneaky-hunter
Fantastic-hider
Colourful creature
Creepy-crawler.

Jessica Magrin (9)
Oak Field Primary School, Gibbonsdown

Jupiter

Stormy-spinner
Giant-racer
Biggest-boulder
Hude-roller
Fast-flyer
Gigantic-swirler.

Josh O'Connell (8)
Oak Field Primary School, Gibbonsdown

Shooting Star

Fast-flyer
Dust-leaver
Ball-boomer
Fire-shooter
Tail-speeder
Rock-burner.

Evelyn North (9)
Oak Field Primary School, Gibbonsdown

Aliens

A haiku

Spaceship invader
Unidentified creature
UFO rider.

Owen Berrow (8)
Oak Field Primary School, Gibbonsdown

The Ocean Growling

Last night, I saw the ocean growling, growling
because it was fierce
Gushing in, rushing out
Rushing like it was in the world Olympics

Last night I saw the ocean was dangerous,
That someone could die
Billowing in, darting out

Last night I saw the sea swell
Like it had broken its finger
Coming in, coming out like a swirling roundabout.

Terah Rose Parkhouse (10)
Shirenewton Primary School, Shirenewton

Space Millionaire

Hi, I'm Toby, I'm a millionaire
I'm nine, I think I'm the youngest in the world.
My friend is John, he is also a millionaire.
He is slightly older than I am.
I want to be the youngest person on the moon,
So I'm making a working rocket.
I am thrilled to be going into space.
The rocket is complete, John and I are getting in.
I am feeling uneasy.
3, 2, 1, lift-off!
We're out of the atmosphere,
We're past the stars.
I'm feeling travel sick but I cannot be sick now.
Zoom! Oh no, another rocket,
We're going to crash.
Boom... crash... Ow!
Ahhhh
Oh, it was only a kind of nice nightmare.

Toby West (10)
St Felix Preparatory School, Reydon

The Firm Foundation

Made of oak 'n' steel,
Stephenson's Rocket a pioneering creation,
1829 a triumphant year,
Made the world a faster place,
A year of new things,
It is a beautiful rolling beast,
Like the painting of the Mona Lisa,
I love how it puffs out smoke like a chimney pot,
The maiden journey so full of joy,
I am sad the age of steam is no more,
No more work for these machines,
37s, 91s, HSTs, TGVs, 153s and 156s,
This was the future,
800s and 755s, bullet trains,
This is the future,
All thanks to one man,
Thank you Mr Stephenson,
You made the world roll.

Samuel Parle (11)
St Felix Preparatory School, Reydon

Bumper Cars

Roaring past the crowd
The race was on
Round the corners
Rocketing past the thin gaps
Between all the competitive drivers
They all knew this was the final lap
Racing past the deafening crowd
Crash! There's been a pile up!
The crowd getting even louder
The pile getting even higher
There was one car standing
It screeched across the track
Melting tyres gave off a revolting smell
The crowd was going wild
What was the driver going to do?
Bang! He hit one of the cars
He soared through the air
Past the chequered flag
He had won!

Henry O'Connor (9)
St Felix Preparatory School, Reydon

Magic

Butterflies flutter in my stomach
I'm feeling nervous
The lights go up, flooding onto the stage
The music starts, booming in my ears
Excited performers chatter all around me
I come out of the smooth red curtain
Magic surrounds me
The lights shining in my eyes
Adrenaline rushing through me like an invisible spirit
I repeat my lines, I repeat my lines
I've rehearsed for hours on end
I dance, I sing
The show ends
The audience clap
I'm in another world
I feel like I belong here
The magic is overwhelming me.

Charlotte Rainer (10)
St Felix Preparatory School, Reydon

My Fussy Friend

Greedier than a pig
My hungry dog Emma.
Lovelier than a dove
My loving dog Emma.
Skinnier than a shrimp
My slim dog Emma.
Feistier than a bull
My strong dog Emma.
As black as coal
My hidden dog Emma.
Rides on the sand
My sloppy dog Emma.
Stays at Nan's
My innocent dog Emma.
Sleeps in her hands
My sleepy dog Emma.
She loves me so
My wonderful dog Emma.
She hates to see me go
My sad dog Emma.
I love her so

My dear dog Emma.
I never want to let her go
My valued dog Emma.

Alex Drake (11)
St Felix Preparatory School, Reydon

Global Warming

The globe is warming and it is turning into a marine landscape
Giant waters overflowing, flooding and engulfing places
Towns and cities being destroyed, people losing their homes
Factory emissions polluting our world, carbons flying from cars
We must stop freeing these toxins into our air
The polar ice caps are melting, forcing wildlife to leave
If we all don't stop this happening now
Our beautiful world's life could end tragically
All these things really, really concern me
What can I do?

Samuel Barker-Harrison (11)
St Felix Preparatory School, Reydon

The Wait

Sleeping and sleeping,
I am snoring so loudly,
The shaking of my bed,
Woken up quite crossly,
I look to my side and to my surprise
I see my grandma and she says, "Hi
Your mum is in the hospital having her baby."
I squeal with excitement,
I jump up and down on my bed,
We drive to my grandma's house
Where we wait for hours and hours.
Finally, the phone rings,
A call to say we can see the baby.
We are there in minutes,
I run into the room
There she lies.

Eva Bullion (10)
St Felix Preparatory School, Reydon

Forest Fires

The crying trees
Dying slowly by the red-hot flames
Licking up their trunks
Animals petrified watching the fires spreading
wildly
Running from the blazing torches
Animals starving, hungry, tired
Planes flying over spitting water
Over flaming branches
Trying to put out the fires
I hate to see trees falling down
I pray every day that it will end
Hoping everything will grow back to normal
Like it was before, like nothing had ever happened.

William Foskett (11)
St Felix Preparatory School, Reydon

Beauties Of Brazil

The rainforest is where the toucans live
We must not give their habitat away
We're destroying the trees they are surrounded by
So don't ever waste paper
Their habitat belongs to them
So we have no right to take it away
They are finding it hard to survive
The birds are being killed and their beaks cut off for jewellery
If this keeps on happening in a few years the toucans will be extinct
I really hope we never ever allow this to happen.

Saffron Vine (11)
St Felix Preparatory School, Reydon

When I Feel Free

The word 'dance' warms my heart.
The music is booming in my ear,
The beat sounds like great fun.
I turn around, my body feels free.
My feet rub along the floor.
I feel like no one's in the room.
I spin round like a roundabout.
It is a challenge and it's fun.
It cheers me up when I am down.
I am so passionate about it, I do it a lot.
I cannot explain how much I love dance.
It is when I feel free.

Grace Cadey (11)
St Felix Preparatory School, Reydon

My Musical Dream

The orchestra is tuning up,
The Albert Hall awaits me.
My nerves are building,
The tune is cheery and bright.
I'm really, really enjoying this,
Oops!
Squeak!
I'm back in my lesson now,
I just can't get this crotchet right.
That's better,
I'm back on track.
Oh no!
I've just played the last note wrong!
I've messed up this tune.
My teacher's looking at me.

John Pitt (9)
St Felix Preparatory School, Reydon

My Amazing Day Out

Skipping excitedly into the woods,
I see a vast deer whizzing past me.
I follow the footpath,
Surrounded by emerald-green grass.
I find a perfect spot to put my picnic down,
With elegant flowers all around.
I have sandwiches, crisps, fruit and drinks,
I'm really hungry and thirsty.
The food is delicious,
I get up from the blanket.
I walk back to the car,
I've had such an incredible time.

Chloe Partridge (10)
St Felix Preparatory School, Reydon

My Big Brother

My brother goes to bed late
But he has to leave by eight.
At home he is moody and rude
Which means he needs some food.
He is addicted to his phone,
Oh you should hear my parents moan.
My brother storms off down the hall,
The doors vibrate but they don't fall.
He goes into his room alone,
Where he says it feels like home.
But I know I will love him more
When he's aged twenty-four.

Bryce Newman (9)
St Felix Preparatory School, Reydon

Skiing

At the top of the slope, a marathon ahead.
With all my might I blast off.
Carving the plastic,
Hitting the poles,
Smash, crash, bash.
A couple of poles left and a diver for the finish.
I look at the timer and I'm winning so far!
Only one more person but he is my enemy.
He takes to the slopes,
Suddenly I hear a big sigh,
He's missed a pole,
I have won!

William Last (10)
St Felix Preparatory School, Reydon

The Dangers Of The Deep

I love what's under the surface of the sea
The fish swimming and undulating about
A hungry octopus sneaking about on the prowl
A school of fish gathering, staying away from a hungry shark
The body of a giant, silent, sunken shipwreck
Its treasure glinting everywhere
A threatening plastic bag floats by
All alone, a vulnerable turtle comes sculling along
The dangers of the deep.

Jude Gunner (10)
St Felix Preparatory School, Reydon

The Exciting Day

I was cleaning the bathroom,
Suddenly my dog ran off,
I went and chased after him.
I ran through the streets,
Where had he gone?
I ran back into my house
In a corner
I saw something,
I went closer,
Warm and muddy.
It was my dog.
I was so relieved,
I thought he would eat me alive.
I played with him all day,
I was so happy
I cried a little.

Jude Groom (10)
St Felix Preparatory School, Reydon

Swimming To The End

I am really nervous
Trembling inside
It is nearly time
It's my first competition I am about to do
I am hoping that I will do well
I know I must believe in myself
I get in and the man says, "Go."
I swim and swim as fast as I can
I am in the lead and that is good
I am nearly there
I get faster and faster
I touch, it's the end and I have won!

Darcey Impson (9)
St Felix Preparatory School, Reydon

The Kindest People In The World

They mean so much to me
Each time they make me smile
Always gentle, loving
Kind and supportive
All the amazing fun holidays together
My family are caring
Fun, thoughtful
Sympathetic, considerate
And of course understanding
I can't say enough about them
I adore my family
We all need family
I could not go on without them
They are my world.

Darcey McDonough (11)
St Felix Preparatory School, Reydon

The Winter Dance

A family outdoor party in winter
Trees covered in snow
My mum and dad dancing to their favourite song
They haven't heard it in very long
Everyone watches them glide across the floor in awe
My entire family gathering onto the floor having a good time
I just watch them in astonishment in front of the beautiful scenery
And I feel as if I am finally home.

Ben Every (11)
St Felix Preparatory School, Reydon

My Dog Called Bob

My dog is called Bob
He is my best friend
He has cute brown eyes
Also shaggy ears
He is ginger behind his ears
He has a black body
His breed is mixed cross terrier
He is as fluffy as a bunny
Also very funny
He does lots of tricks
He loves me
Also I love him
And we make a great team together.

Holly Wilson (9)
St Felix Preparatory School, Reydon

UFO

UFO you like to say it
Unless you fall into a great pit
What a wonderful day you might say
Until you look up...
And say...
What is that, I don't like that
I don't think I should give it a pat
I looked down, I saw a green and clean thing
With big eyes, fat lies
You think what to do
You might go to the zoo
This mysterious creature isn't a leech
Or your everyday creature
You call 999, don't know what to do
You're thinking what will the alien do
Police come with their diamond-blue sirens
The emerald-green alien runs away
I follow it and I go to a hideout
I see lots of aliens and say I'm out
I come in more and become friends
I hope they like to lend

I grab a laser blaster 1,000,000
And blast the police to my friend
I wake up with fear and realise I'm clear
I look on the clock, oh that's a lot
It's twelve o'clock
Was it a nightmare or a dream
I go to sleep...
Boom! More fear?

Mike Tomlein (9)
St Michael & St John's RC Primary School, Clitheroe

My Favourite Time Of Year

My favourite time of year
Is nearly here
Cake, presents, bring all the joy and fun
My chocolate cake is nearly done
When I woke up I jumped out of bed
I ran upstairs and bumped my head
Mum and Dad woke up with a jolt
And got my presents
I sat in their bed all cosy and warm
To start opening my presents
On the way was a swarm of fun.

Sofia Roche (7)
Stifford Clays Primary School, Stifford Clays

Mars

This is a poem about Mars
Where they don't have cars
They walk about on six feet
And eat lots and lots of meat
You see aliens live on this land
Where it's very red and full of sand
They have six feet and use them all
Because they don't have any cars on Mars.

Iris Clark (8)
Stifford Clays Primary School, Stifford Clays

Family Planets

Girls go to college to get more knowledge
Boys go to Jupiter to get more stupider
Mum goes to Mars to get a bigger vase
Dad goes to Spain to get a bigger brain
Baby needs the restroom so we stop off at Neptune
We go to the moon right after Neptune.

Lily Yuen (7)
Stifford Clays Primary School, Stifford Clays

A Galaxy Verse

The universe is a never-ending space
I wonder if it holds another race
It is not a difficult thing to see
They could be in a different galaxy.

Ava Coldwell (7)
Stifford Clays Primary School, Stifford Clays

A Star Shines

A poor little star was the loner of the gang
Little and lonely she felt a pang
"Oh I feel so sad," she cried
Suddenly the lost little star had a blast of pride
Then she realised it was the saviour of the night
She saw the mighty sun say oh little star
Take a moment to look around
Although you are different every star can shine
Realisation hit the star and she knew
She had to find her friends
She followed the great shining star
Helping her find her way back to her pack
Is this fate for the little star?
Now she is back with friends
Each star realises that they can lend
Some help for every star to mend.

Olivia O'Brien (11)
Twycross House School, Twycross

A Dream That Comes To Life

Aliens move around my head
I dream this dream as I lie in bed
The spaceships: the white, the green, the red
They swarm all around my bed
I sit up and see
It is not what it appears to be
A princess sleeping on the floor
A knight is creeping through the door
I cannot believe what is happening
The next moment the knight is pulling out a ring
It's big, it's white, it's crystal clear
It looks like a big dramatic sphere
They vanish at once
A wizard appears
His cone hat covers his ginormous ears
He says, "Abracadabra" and "Whoopee dee doo"
This world is imaginative, fantastic and new
I then hear a shout
It's my mother without a doubt

I said, "Vanish at once" and off everything goes
Then I climb into bed and feel my heart glow.

Martha Bettley (11) & Victoria Hudson
Twycross House School, Twycross

They're Not Extinct

Many people think dinosaurs died
But the secret is (if I'm obliged)
Dinosaurs simply flew to space
To a special place
The moon, don't believe me okay
The only thing I did was go out of my way to say
They play on the craters bouncing up and down
One dinosaur drinks pink Pepsi out of a magical moon cup
Yes all of them are there, stegosaurus, T-rexes
They're so glad they got away from Brexit
Who knows the next animals that will go to the moon
Maybe baboons.

Alessandra Beck (11)
Twycross House School, Twycross

The Fatal Day Of The Dinosaurs

They were around millions of years ago
Then the asteroids made them go
The distressing sounds of the dying
As their friends started crying

The dinosaurs roamed the earth
Until that fatal day
They loved to play
Till that day
When they were made to go away

But maybe
They're destined to return
One hopeful wish is made
Until they return to the stage
But till that day we say goodbye
We sure do hope time will fly.

Isabelle Randle (10)
Twycross House School, Twycross

Moon Dinosaur

M y family is gone, I'm all alone
O verwhelmed with grief
O utrageous sadness
N ow I just feel obliged to cry

D on't cry, I told myself
I may not be the only one
N o harm in snooping round
O h look over there
S omewhere over there
A creature, a green dotted thing
U nder a pile of magical moon dust
R oar! It's another dinosaur.

Violet Stacey (11)
Twycross House School, Twycross

To Be An Astronaut

I'd love to be an astronaut
Flying through the air without a thought
Soaring past planets and stars so bright
Giving the aliens a fright
Seeing comets and asteroids
Taking photos with my space droids
Saturn with her beautiful rings
Made of ice, rock and other things
Going to another solar system
Without my family I really miss them
I've trodden on all kinds of turf
But none as good as that of Earth.

Scarlett Tombs (11)
Twycross House School, Twycross

Out Of This World!

R oaming out of this world
O ur rocket swirled and twirled
C razy aliens dancing, making me glad
K aleidoscope colours are driving me mad
E xtremely close we are at last
T ons of planets passing fast
S tars are quickly whizzing past, so now it's time to slow it down, setting ourselves back on the ground.

Amelia Carthy
Twycross House School, Twycross

Aliens

Aliens in their spaceships so bright
Love to fly across the night
Oh what a wonderful sight
This is an alien delight
The spaceships look like they are alight
Although we aliens do not bite.

Clara Taviner-Hodge (10)
Twycross House School, Twycross

Miss Bates Our Teacher

Our teacher is as sporty as an athlete,
She dances like a swan,
She is as bendy as a gummy sweet,
She is clever like Einstein and never gets things wrong.

She is as bouncy as a volleyball,
She is as brave as a lioness,
She is like a rockstar which is very cool,
She is organised like a library and never makes a mess.

Our teacher is as spectacular as the universe,
She is as rare as a rainbow dolphin,
She is as caring as a friendly nurse,
She is funny like a comedian and always makes us grin.

Our teacher is inspiring like Rosa Parks,
She is as wonderful as a shining star,
She is as fierce as a school of sharks,
She is as sweet as a Galaxy bar.

Our teacher is as fast as a cheetah,
She is as quick-witted as a magician,
She warms up the classroom like a heater,
She is like a friend willing to learn.

She is as beautiful as a shiny new pearl,
She is as strong as a the Hulk,
She is like a ballerina and loves to twirl,
Unlike the Hulk, she never likes to sulk.

Our teacher is as bright as the sun,
She is like a deep sea diver,
Her brain is like a dictionary full of lots of fun,
She is like a soldier, a true survivor.

This is why we all love her!

Sycamore Class
Walgrave Primary School, Walgrave

Best Friends

Our friendship is so strong
Other people make fun of it
At least we get along
We can never ever be split

Whenever you're down
You can count on me
So don't go and drown
Or get lost in the deep blue sea

We are both sporty and lazy
In our own way
We are both really crazy
We are the perfect match hooray

Your house is big, mine is small
You get things right
I get things wrong
You are small, I am tall
No matter the differences
We still get along.

Lily Knight (10)
Walgrave Primary School, Walgrave

Me

J oseph loves jogging
O utstanding like an alien
S tructures are my thing
E xcited is what I get a lot
P ing pong I'm not good
H ang, hang, no I'll fall off

L unch is what I like a lot
U nderground I like to pound
D igging in the dirt you're not a twirp
W ashing in water I don't think is a slaughter
I nk I don't think it does stink
G irls are not in our gang.

Joseph Ludwig (9)
Walgrave Primary School, Walgrave

Best Ship

Our friendship will never break, unlike others
We will always be best friends
Sometimes we fall out
But we are best friends forever
Most people moan and moan with each other
People fight with each other
But we will be best friends forever and ever

Some people will break your heart
If so then ignore them and walk away
You and me will be there for each other
People will tear you down
But we are best friends forever.

Sophie Holmes (9)
Walgrave Primary School, Walgrave

Our Friendship

Our friendship will never end
Our friendship is the best
Our friendship will stay strong
Unlike others we will stay together

Stay together forever
Never worry, we have each other
Whenever you're in trouble, call me
You know I will always come

Our friendship is forever
Our friendship is stronger than others
Our friendship is never going to end
We will never forget each other.

Ellie Brown (10)
Walgrave Primary School, Walgrave

The Thing

Teeth dark like coal
A deep darkening soul
Hair as spiky as thorns
Hands as cold as corn
Its body as big as a king-sized bed
It makes you want to put
The covers on your head
It lets out a big furious roar
It should get arrested for breaking the law
Feet as big as doors
As they're banging on the floors.

Harvey Singh Hammond (9)
Walgrave Primary School, Walgrave

Four Seasons

Summer is the season of blooming
The bees are always consuming
Butterflies elegantly flutter away
Their beautiful wings in a sway

Winter is the season of coldness
People cuddle up in the warmness
Sometimes the weather muddles up
And curls up like a cup

Autumn is the season of fall
Wind blows in the hall
Whilst crows are joining in
As if to find a pin

Summer is the season of the sun
Usually it's so much fun
In my opinion it's number one
As it has been such an amazing time.

Manal Mohamed Hilmy (10)
Weald Rise Primary School, Harrow Weald

The Amazing Four Seasons

Winter is the season of snow
Really strong winds blow
I think it is great
Some people have feelings of hate

In autumn the leaves fall down
All the way to the ground
Children playing happily with leaves
That crunch like granola in herbs

The season of hotness is summer
It is amazing like a runner
Trotting in the lovely summer breeze
As the buffalo stampede

Let us talk about spring
Which Mother Nature will bring
This lovely flowery time to the brim
Not at all grim.

Shamsa Abdalla (10)
Weald Rise Primary School, Harrow Weald

What Happens To Space?

Let me introduce you to space
Where the stars all race
It is not a quiet place
Like to meet new planets face to face?

Not to mention that random shoelace
You are the bait for a big alien chase
Bury your eyes if they're near
As they talk just block your ears

You will be put in a coma
If you don't smell the sweet aroma
Ask the planets what happened to the deer
They say he betrayed me right here.

Patricia Sterchevici (9)
Weald Rise Primary School, Harrow Weald

Snowflake

Snowflake, snowflake falling down
Touching the ground as if a crown
I wonder what is up there?
Shiny and glittery like a glare

A colossal pool of shimmering glitter
On my glass and glove they flicker
Could not believe what happened
As the grass got saddened

White, shimmery, glamourous snowman
That turns into an iron man
Only to melt down
As we all end up in a frown.

Khadeeja Fairoos (10)
Weald Rise Primary School, Harrow Weald

Amazing Animals

Great and many in number
Sweet like a pot of sugar
As we look, laugh and play
Animals are having their way

Autumn leaves crunch under their feet
Many more creatures you would like to meet
From soft and cosy to vile and tough
I like gentle and you may like rough

Cool, scary and fierce, yet very smart
Most with a very gentle heart.

Rikza Mohamed Mohamed Rikas (9)
Weald Rise Primary School, Harrow Weald

Planet Mars

Glaring at shimmering Mars
The twinkling stars mesmerised me
Hovering around the planet
Producing the most amazing sounds

Boiling Mars is no joke
Seems heavy like a yoke
All in the night
Mars has lots of sights

As the sun comes up
Mars gets a sup
How Mars has luck
To frolic like a duck.

Ayesha Mohamed Fairoos (8)
Weald Rise Primary School, Harrow Weald

Titanic - Is This Happening?

Down the grand staircase I came,
My head was really in pain,
Threw my shoes off,
Pulled on my socks,
Lay exhausted on my bed,
Pressed a cold towel on my aching head,
It was late...
Someone came in with a latte,
And potty,
Time to go out for the night.
Got myself ready,
With high heels,
Ohhhh steady!
Then while I was eating,
I heard a scrape,
I ran to my cabin,
Slipping on a napkin,
Looked out my porthole,
Then I saw an iceberg!

Katelyn Beaumont (9)
Ysgol Borthyn, Ruthin

Rainbows

Rainbows are red like summer roses,
Rainbows are orange like crunchy carrots,
Rainbows are yellow like the flaming sun,
Rainbows are colourful,
Rainbows are cool,
Rainbows are green like wavy grass,
Rainbows are blue like the cloudy sky,
Rainbows are purple like misty lavender,
Rainbows can be three colours, sometimes seven,
Rainbows are beautiful reaching up to Heaven.

Caitlyn Spencer (9)
Ysgol Borthyn, Ruthin

Serena The Confident Star

Out in the big black space,
There is one small place,
Where there is a bright little star,
With the space around her as black as char.

She likes to eat moon rocks,
And for a drink,
She likes it pink.

She, I say, is confident,
She shines like a star,
But her hair is as bright as a new car.

When it's the end of the day,
She will forever stay,
In her sparkly, confident way.

Jasmine Rose Murray (9)
Ysgol Bro Aled, Llansannan

Does My Family Really Know Best?

School days are the best days of your life,
So my family say to me.
But do they really understand?
I'm there from nine till three!
My family say that work is tough,
They work early till late.
That means sometimes they are up all night,
But to me that sounds great!
I go to school and see my friends
I learn new things, I learn new trends.
Sometimes there are parties, sometimes pantomimes
Yet my favourite part of the day is break times!
But it is really hard going to school,
I have to get up at eight!
Playing sports and doing activities with all of my classmates,
Me and my friends all feel the same,
Going to school is tough!
We want to stay in bed and game,

But Mum says I game too much!
They say I get lots of holidays
And it's not the same for them.
Six weeks off in summer,
Now that is a little gem!

Okay...
As I write this I realise,
Being young is ace!
School is more fun than I thought
It's not such a bad place!

Alfie Howells (11)
Ysgol Cae'r Nant, Connahs Quay

A Busy Little Bee...

I am a bee, a buzzy little bee
Nobody cares about me

I flutter around all day long
Pollinating flowers and buzzing along

I collect nectar and pollen for my hive
Keeping the circle of life alive!

Bet you didn't know, a third of food you eat
Depends on me, now that's hard to beat!

You waft me away, treat me so mean
'A nuisance' I am but to nature I'm queen

Keep going, treat me this way
You will find no food to eat one day...

Screaming and flapping and swatting me dead
You'll be sorry when you're not fed

A world without bees is not a world at all
But a world without humans will flourish above all!

Holly Crossley (11)
Ysgol Cae'r Nant, Connahs Quay

Up Above

In the dark I look above and what do I see?
Planes flying free and birds in the tree,
Candyfloss clouds in the blue sky,
And the sun gleaming in my eye.

In the night I look above and what do I see?
Stars in the galaxy shining for me,
And now a wave from the man in the moon,
As I go to bed an hour too soon.

Ella Leverton (10)
Ysgol Cae'r Nant, Connahs Quay

The Solar System

S pace is super,
O ut there is amazing,
L ots of fun for everyone!
A re you brave enough to try?
R eady to go on this amazing adventure?

S hut the door tight,
Y ou're about to take off.
S trap on your seat belts,
T he countdown has begun.
E veryone, let's have some fun and
M ake magical memories!

Jennifer Lewis (8)
Ysgol Garth Olwg, Church Village

The Shiniest Star

I look up and spot the shiniest star,
Up, up, up high in the dark sky,
How you twinkle and glitter ever so high,
I see, I listen, I gaze at you,
Looking at the patterns all around,
Creating a beautiful, peaceful sound,
How my mind drifts to all the times we've shared,
The fun, the giggles and how you cared,
I really miss you every day, but when
I look up high, high in the sky,
You are the most shiniest star
And I do not cry...

Ffion-Jane Enoch
Ysgol Gynradd Gymraeg Caerffili, Caerphilly

Cold Space

Space, cold, cold space. A mysterious place! It goes on forever and like every mystery people ask questions that no one can answer.
In the middle of space is me, shot out from the spaceship of Apollo 155, a failed experiment, and now I am waiting and floating for my pick-up to come and save me, if they don't think I'm dead that is!
It's quite peaceful in space, no sounds, no movement, only the stars and the planets to keep me company. Only yesterday I floated past the moon and now it's gone.
Now I am staring at the rocky, red surface of Mars, my oxygen tank is really low. Someone better come soon...
I'm checking my helmet and my heart skips a beat. It is a spaceship! They have finally come for me! Oh wait, it's just rubble from a spaceship!
I am breathing as slow as ever now, saving oxygen and looking at the biggest planet in our solar system - Jupiter! Now the hot planet with its cold rings - Saturn!

A massive ship has come into view. It shoots out a claw, grabs me and yanks me towards it. I am saved! I look back and say goodbye to the cold, cold space.

Roan Oakley (11)
Ysgol Llywelyn, Rhyl

Moon Cheese

I climbed in my rocket to get myself to space
But what I saw will spread laughter across the human race

As I landed on the moon I got out my rocket
What I saw made my eyes jump out of their sockets!

I saw aliens, I saw so many
But I can't tell you how many not for any penny!

The reason for this, I'll tell you now
I couldn't count how many, no matter how!

Each of them looked at me dead in the eye
Quite literally 'dead', I thought I would die!

One of the aliens came over to me, smiled and said "Want some moon cheese?"

He put some on display and I said, "From what shelf?"
He looked at me, smiled again and said, "Help yourself!"

He said, "Honestly, I don't mind, have as much as you please
Sit down and have some moon cheese!"

Kayleigh Roberts (11)
Ysgol Llywelyn, Rhyl

The Silent Voice

I'm in my spaceship zooming to space
I can't see anything, my mind's gone blank
I can hear a whisper but I cannot see it
I think to myself, *what could it be?*
I'm under attack, I need to escape
I rush to the door and open the flap
The voice gets louder but I cannot see it
I feel like I'm frozen, I cannot move
I believe in myself, I need to flee
What is it? What is it that's after me?
Counting down I get ready to jump, all of a sudden the voice stops
All of a sudden I can see again but my memories have gone
What happened to me?
Is it a dream? Is it all real?
Then I wake up and my room is dark
I switch on the light and I realise it was just a dream.

Olivia Muller (10)
Ysgol Llywelyn, Rhyl

Space Nerves

Space is full of galaxies, containing stars and planets with no gravity
The stars shine bright with the Northern Lights
Depending on the weather with help from the satellite
There are eight planets in the solar system
Four rocky planets, two gas giants, two ice planets
And only two of the planets have rings
When a rocket blasts off it creates thrusts
Which blocks the view of the atmosphere
And the SpaceX creator Elon Musk
Russia and the US competed in the space race
Storming through the sky
Looking out at all the brightest stars in the Milky Way.

Emma Watkiss (11)
Ysgol Llywelyn, Rhyl

The Planets In Our Solar System

In our solar system the planets are:
Mercury, Venus, Earth, Mars, Jupiter, Saturn, Uranus, and Neptune
Mercury is a very yellow colour and Venus is a yellow gold colour
The Earth is blue and green
Mars is red and orange
Jupiter is white and orange and peach
Saturn is orange, yellow and has a grey ring around it
Uranus is a really light blue with a white ring around it
Neptune is dark blue and has a white ring around it
These are the colours of the planets and the sun is the yellow king.

Evie Collier (10)
Ysgol Llywelyn, Rhyl

Saturn Is Cool And Hot

S aturn's rings are so cold you can see snow, there it is, just let it go
P opular colour orange, I know that's what colour Saturn is, not forgetting yellow, that's what colour Saturn is, I know
A t night, 62 moons hover round Saturn because that's how many moons go round Saturn
C ould there be 62 rings around Saturn? Should we find out? Come on, let's find out
E veryone knows, well not everyone, is Mars a gas planet? Come on, let's find out...

Callum Mannion (11)
Ysgol Llywelyn, Rhyl

Asteroids

A steroids zooming around
S ometimes might be small from the distance but it rules
T ime stops at twelve, then goes back to five when the asteroid hits
E choes all around because of the loud asteroids
R oaring through the air like a tornado
O r like a rocket, so hard it won't make a crack
I see a giant rocky ball that's big
D on't set foot on one or it will burn badly.

Ruby Hartley (11)
Ysgol Llywelyn, Rhyl

Starlight

S tars are brightening up the sky
T hese amazing stars are so high
A lthough they look so near
R eally they are far from here
L ighting up the sky is a shooting star
I t goes so fast nobody can beat you in the car
G oing so fast, making people's dreams come true
H opefully your dreams come true
T his beautiful star is really rare so make your wish come true.

Teagan Jones (11)
Ysgol Llywelyn, Rhyl

Aliens Vs Earthlings

Aliens came to Earth
To reclaim their victory
At the current war
"Give us our victory!"
The aliens chanted
"Give us our victory!"
Earthlings denied
"End this war!"
"It's against the law!"
Aliens put the Earthlings
Into their rocketship
And they sailed away
Into outer space
And were gone
Without a trace!

Lucy Bamford (11)
Ysgol Llywelyn, Rhyl

Planets

J upiter is a glamorous planet
U ranus is a cold planet
P luto is a nice little planet up in space
I n space, or the galaxy you may call it, lay tons of stars and planets
T itan is a moon, not many people know a lot about it
E arth is the loved planet, every person on Earth knows it!
R ockets go into space to investigate planets.

Madison Parr (10)
Ysgol Llywelyn, Rhyl

The Mysterious Planet

Have you heard about Zippity Zop Zop Zop?
It's the new planet in our solar system
Don't stick a pin in it, it will pop!
Its old system kicked it out, the system called the solar system

Oh, I forgot, there is another life form on it
The planet alone has 5,000 moons
A human is going there in a little bit
Every alien that is there listens to tunes.

Bailey Ellis (10)
Ysgol Llywelyn, Rhyl

A Super Star

S tars, they are small, well... thanks to us they are huge
T his poem is about a cute baby star
A star that wants to come to Earth and be just like a human
R eally, he is desperate to come to us and see how we live with gravity
S ee how we send rockets into space with gravity. But he knows he can't, he is a star, a super star!

Josh Hamilton (11)
Ysgol Llywelyn, Rhyl

Samantha Saturn

He ring iced with diamonds and gems
She wears a necklace of ice in the shape of 'm's
Her face smiling all day, going round and round
Nothing up there is making a sound

Her yellowish town, she's twins with the sun
Anyone who goes there their bodies will go numb
I don't know about you but I don't want to go to Saturn!

Mia Jones (11)
Ysgol Llywelyn, Rhyl

The Space Monster

The space monster hunts for flesh
The space monster loves cooked meat
The space monster's legs like to leave tracks
The space monster's head hates angry animals
The space monster's hands are aggressive
The space monster's weapons love crushing animals
The space monster likes taking over our mind
What if it's me?

Jake Lamb (10)
Ysgol Llywelyn, Rhyl

Earthlings

Strange place this
Their inhabitants are rooted to the spot
I say hello, they ignore me, quite rude!
A group of ugly, disgusting things come near me
I have to run before they see me!

Warren Wold (10)
Ysgol Llywelyn, Rhyl

Purple City

There was this planet called the Purple City
There were aliens living on it
It was really cold
If you tried to land on it you would freeze
There were a lot of aliens living on it!

Huw Espley (11)
Ysgol Llywelyn, Rhyl

Space! Space! Space!

A rocket goes up... whoosh!
Up, up to space
The atmosphere is solemn
Only up in space
We are in the Milky Way
Space! Space! Space!

Mars is as red as the sun
Earth is as blue as Neptune
All except for the smallest one
Pluto!
We are in the Milky Way
Space! Space! Space!

Jupiter has a storm
Saturn has a belt
Uranus has a ring
Neptune is the last one
We are in the Milky Way
Space! Space! Space!

I can smell fuel from the rockets
I can smell cold comets and enormous asteroids

I can see the storms on Jupiter
I can taste astronaut's ice cream
We are in the Milky Way
Space! Space! Space!

Mercury is the closest to the sun
Venus is the hottest one
Rockets go up, down, left, right
We are in the Milky Way.

Nia Benson (11)
Ysgol Melyd, Prestatyn

My Rapid Puppy

My puppy is a crazy kisser
Especially on your return home!
He runs around
And gives you his bone
Bone, bone, bone

When he returns
He brings some love
To anyone who is his buddy
Offering a huggy

Food time
It smells like poo
It's very gooey and gloopy
But it is gone in one gulp!

Walking time
I let him go
He chases rabbits
He gets faster, oh no
I miss a heartbeat
When it squeals

When we're home
He has the toy
He is like a lawnmower
It squeaks loud
My ears are like fireworks exploding inside

When it's bedtime
He is outside (having a wee)
Upstairs in bed I'm as snug as a rug
Ready for him to come and hug.

Benjamin Hannah (10)
Ysgol Melyd, Prestatyn

Eurofighter Typhoon

Excellent jet zooms through the sky
Ultimate and loud, that is what I love
Rhyl is the place, I watch it
Oh wow, very noisy indeed
Flying through the sky
It comes from one side, I wonder where
Giant exhaust shows us the fire
Happy I feel when I see this sight
To the airshow I go
Exciting sight it is
Roars through the sky
Terrific sound I love to hear
You can see it in August
Powerful jet, come and see
"How fast does it go?" I ask my dad
Oh wow! That is fast, fast, fast and furious
Oh, how I love the noise of the jet
Now it is my favourite jet!

Ethan Duffy Hamill (10)
Ysgol Melyd, Prestatyn

Panda Party

All my panda pals are here
Let's all party and cheer
Should we go to the park?
No way, it's too dark
I smell delicious cake
Oh, you're late, cool Cate!
This party is as fun as Flip Out
We love Monopoly
We hate broccoli
Party, party, party!

The banging music in my ear
The taste of candyfloss dissolving on my tongue
I can feel the magic of the pool
I can see all of my fantastic friends
Bang goes the pots and pans!
Crash go the baby cots
Snap goes the lamp
Oh no, my new dress!
My house is a mess
Party, party, party!

Violet O'Neill (9)
Ysgol Melyd, Prestatyn

Wolves

W olves howling at the moon
O h how cute they are
N ext to the caves they live
D ark in the night they attack
E ating fresh meat
R abbits are what the wolves see
F oxes are what they see
U nique taste of food
L ovely fur when I touch it

W onderful hearing like a dog
O h my cute little wolf teddy
L icking my face
V iolent attacks throughout the night
E ating some mushrooms
S leeping in the day and sometimes in the night - wolves, wolves, wolves.

Summer Eastwood (11)
Ysgol Melyd, Prestatyn

Helpless Space

Up, up, up in helpless space
Such a massive, yet quiet place,
Everywhere you look it's blinding light
I see the stars twinkling bright!

I see the sun scorching hot
Will I burn? Oh, I hope not!
I see the sun, I feel the heavy heat
I think my heart just skipped a beat... *bang!*

I hear the roars of Earth below
Is it time to go home? I think so,
I hop into my rocket feeling proud
As I shoot down through the clouds... *whoosh!*

Lily Adams (10)
Ysgol Melyd, Prestatyn

My Teacher

Marvellous marking
Beautiful being
Busy bee
Comfy clothing
Comical glasses
School glasses
Learning, here I come!

Incredible imagination
Luminously loud
Precious perfume
Superior singing
Satisfied sports
Terrific topics
School glasses
Learning, here I come!

Fantastic foody
Various voices
School glasses
Learning, here I come!

She is like my mum
Her classes are always fun
But what she is... is my teacher!

Natarlia Stojkovska (11)
Ysgol Melyd, Prestatyn

My Dog Arlo

Attention addict
Brave barker
Ruff - woah!
Carpet crumpler
Food gobbler
Fluffy friend
Grass gobbler
Kennel craver
Keen walker
Ladies' man
Mountain marcher
Rapid racer
Super sleeper
Toy chewer
Water chugger
Whoosh wannabe
Oh how I love
My dog Arlo.

Ben Hughes (11)
Ysgol Melyd, Prestatyn

Winter/Christmas

Winter wonderland
Frost falling
Slippy snow
Snow globe
Jack Frost
Carol-singers
Fluffy snow
Snow fights
Good sights
Hot chocolate
Mince pies
Freezing weather
Hats, scarves
Cats, gloves
Bible reader
Funfair
Hot drinks

Bella Bennett (10)
Ysgol Melyd, Prestatyn

My Lovely Dog Nala Wala Woo

Attention-seeker
Energy-taker
Fast-walker
Friend-maker
Food-eater
Head-acher
Loud-barker
Mess-maker
Messy-scratcher
Noise-giver
Toy-chewer
Treat-lover
Water-liker
My dog is an ancient, unique animal!

Theo Haywood (10)
Ysgol Melyd, Prestatyn

Westies

Always trumping
Annoying barker
Ball shredder
Fence jumper
Grass flicker
Hand biter
Loud howler
Loves eating
Loves licking
Very loyal
Super fluffy
Teddy chewer
Very mischievous
Hole digger.

Oliver Aspinwall (11)
Ysgol Melyd, Prestatyn

Winter

Wet winter
Hot chocolate
Freezing Friday
Perfect presents
Super Santa
Friends, family
Red reindeer
Satisfying stocking
Rog robot
Chilling chocolate
Silly, stinky.

Iwan Miles (10)
Ysgol Melyd, Prestatyn

Family Members

F abulous fashion
A m wishing the best for you
M agnificent parenting
I will always be there for you
L oyalty passes on
Y es, we made it to the end.

Louis Jones (10)
Ysgol Melyd, Prestatyn

The Change

Aliens playing happily on Planet Shock
That shines like a disco ball,
The aliens look like little dogs
Who always surprised us all!

Disturbed by some noises, the aliens looked,
They saw something weird and pale,
But as they got closer he was colourful;
And they were disappointed it wasn't Gareth Bale!

After a while they all calmed down,
They saw that he was only human
One alien said, "This is my time to shine!
I have decided to become a man!"

He remembered the button that was on his jumper
And wanted to change and press it right now,
He then pressed the button and magically
He changed into a man and everybody said,
"Wow!"

Isobel Jane Pellew (11)
Ysgol Pum Heol, Llanelli

Into The Solar System

We're off into space, a trip to the stars
In to the rocket ship quick, first stop is Mars
5, 4, 3, 2, 1... butterflies in my tum
Feel the engines starting up, here we come
Sling-shotting around the moon
Don't worry, Mummy, I will be home soon
Jupiter gigantic, the rings of Saturn next
I feel like Captain Kirk in the film 'Star Trek'!
Meteors, asteroids, the burning hot sun
Now I am heading back home, space trip done!

Oliver Manning (8)
Ysgol Pum Heol, Llanelli

You Were Right, This Is Out Of This World

Shooting out of the sky
Purple and blue colours flashing
A bus appeared with space creatures inside
I hopped onto the bus, it flew me to another universe
Space Town
There were astronauts and aliens
They were looking for the children
Rockets smashing everything, everything was floating
Space Town is the weirdest world, a world in a faraway orbit
Was I dreaming?
Suddenly I woke up
I saw all the creatures floating in my room
Was it real or was I dreaming?
But I knew I wasn't
Because I always believe
So I joined the creatures

Then suddenly...
"Breakfast time!"
Cadi Fflur DeSouza (11)
Ysgol Pum Heol, Llanelli

Moon Limerick

There was a young man called Sir Spoon
Who spent all his life on the moon
He ate some strange cheese
And got lost in the seas
And said, "I hope a spaceship comes soon!"

Eiry Bailey (8)
Ysgol Pum Heol, Llanelli

The World

The world is dying but nobody knows
No one believes us because we are young
New Zealand dealing with smoke and Australia with fire
But I still have hope and desire
People are killing the Earth
With plastic and pollution
But I really do hope they will find a solution
The world is flashing before our eyes
Before we know it we will say goodbye
Australia is on fire, just like the sun
The world is dying, oh what have we done?
Climate is changing, nobody cares
Ice is melting, nobody cares
Global warming is expected, there is no hope
For the last time, it is not a joke!

Silvija Liuzinaite (11)
Ysgol Wepre School, Connah's Quay

Special Seasons

Haiku poetry

Spring is coming fast
Bluebell heads peep sleepily
New life will emerge

Love is in the air
Valentine's Day is coming
Chocolates being bought

Snow falls from the sky
People get excited fast
Snow will come quite soon.

Charlotte Sprake (11)
Ysgol Wepre School, Connah's Quay

Koalas In Australia

Koalas are dying,
What can we do?
They matter just as much as me and you,
The fire is burning,
Their fur is falling,
They are crying for help,
But no one hears them yelp!

Sebastian Randles (11)
Ysgol Wepre School, Connah's Quay

YOUNG WRITERS INFORMATION

We hope you have enjoyed reading this book – and that you will continue to in the coming years.

If you're a young writer who enjoys reading and creative writing, or the parent of an enthusiastic poet or story writer, do visit our website **www.youngwriters.co.uk**. Here you will find free competitions, workshops and games, as well as recommended reads, a poetry glossary and our blog. There's lots to keep budding writers motivated to write!

If you would like to order further copies of this book, or any of our other titles, then please give us a call or order via your online account.

Young Writers
Remus House
Coltsfoot Drive
Peterborough
PE2 9BF
(01733) 890066
info@youngwriters.co.uk

Join in the conversation!
Tips, news, giveaways and much more!

YoungWritersUK   @YoungWritersCW

Alright Sin, I'll share Void with you.

How does alternating weekends sound?

(I get Christmas)